NBA CHAMPIONSHIPS:

NONE

ALL-TIME LEADING SCORER:

DAVID WEST (2003–11):

8,690 POINTS

THE NBA:
A HISTORY
OF HOOPS

NEW ORLEANS
PELICANS

PELICA

THE NBA: A HISTORY OF HOOPS

NEW ORLEANS PELICANS

BY JIM WHITING

CREATIVE EDUCATION CREATIVE PAPERBACKS

Published by Creative Education
and Creative Paperbacks

P.O. Box 227, Mankato, Minnesota 56002

Creative Education and Creative Paperbacks
are imprints of The Creative Company

www.thecreativecompany.us

Design and production by Blue Design

Printed in the United States of America

Photographs by AP Images (ASSOCIATED PRESS), Corbis (Steve Lipofsky), Getty Images (Nathaniel S. Butler/NBAE, Ronald Cortes/Getty Images Sport, James Drake/Sports Illustrated, Chris Graythen, Chris Graythen/NBAE, Jim Gund, Hiroyuki Matsumoto, Michael Ochs Archives, Layne Murdoch/NBAE, Tom Pennington/Getty Images Sport, Doug Pensinger/Getty Images Sport, Stacy Revere/Getty Images Sport, Bob Rosato/Sports Illustrated, Kent Worner/NBAE), Newscom (MIKE BROWN/EFE, Ron Jenkins/MCT, Stephen Lew/Icon Sportswire, Albert Pena/Icon SMI)

Library of Congress Cataloging-in-Publication Data

Names: Whiting, Jim, 1943- author.

Title: New Orleans Pelicans / Jim Whiting.

Series: The NBA: A History of Hoops.

Includes bibliographical references and index.

Summary: This high-interest title summarizes the history of the New Orleans Pelicans professional basketball team, highlighting memorable events and noteworthy players such as Anthony Davis.

Identifiers: LCCN 2017005590 / ISBN 978-1-60818-853-6 (hardcover) / ISBN 978-1-62832-456-3 (pbk) / ISBN 978-1-56660-901-2 (eBook)

Subjects: LCSH: 1. New Orleans Pelicans (Basketball team)—History—Juvenile literature. 2. New Orleans Pelicans (Basketball team)—Biography—Juvenile literature.

Classification: LCC GV885.52.N376 W55 2017 / DDC 796.323/640976335—dc23

CCSS: RI.4.1, 2, 3, 4; RI.5.1, 2, 4; RI.6.1, 2, 3; RF.4.3, 4; RF.5.3, 4; RH. 6-8. 4, 5, 7

First Edition HC 9 8 7 6 5 4 3 2 1

First Edition PBK 9 8 7 6 5 4 3 2 1

SPALDING

WARRIORS

CONTENTS

Nicknamed "The Big Easy," **NEW ORLEANS** is known for jazz music and Mardi Gras.

HONORING MUSICAL ROOTS

The Houston Rockets roared into New Orleans on January 2, 2015. The Rockets were on their way to clinching a high National Basketball Association (NBA) playoff seed. Superstar guard James Harden routinely threw down 30 or 40 points a game. The New Orleans Pelicans, on the other hand, were a young team. The players were still finding their way. But that night, Houston had a problem. A big problem. Harden scored just 11 points. The Pelicans powered to a 59–42 halftime lead.

They wanted more. "We brought it in the huddle and just said, 'Keep putting the pressure on them, don't stop being aggressive,'" said shooting guard Tyreke Evans. "We did that." Houston coach Kevin McHale agreed. "We were terrible tonight. They came out and just kicked our tails up one side and down the other." McHale knew the game was over. He sat his starters early in the third quarter. New Orleans coach Monty Williams did the same thing in the fourth quarter. If he hadn't, the beatdown probably would been even greater than the 111–83 final score. "We made the right plays defensively, and it led to

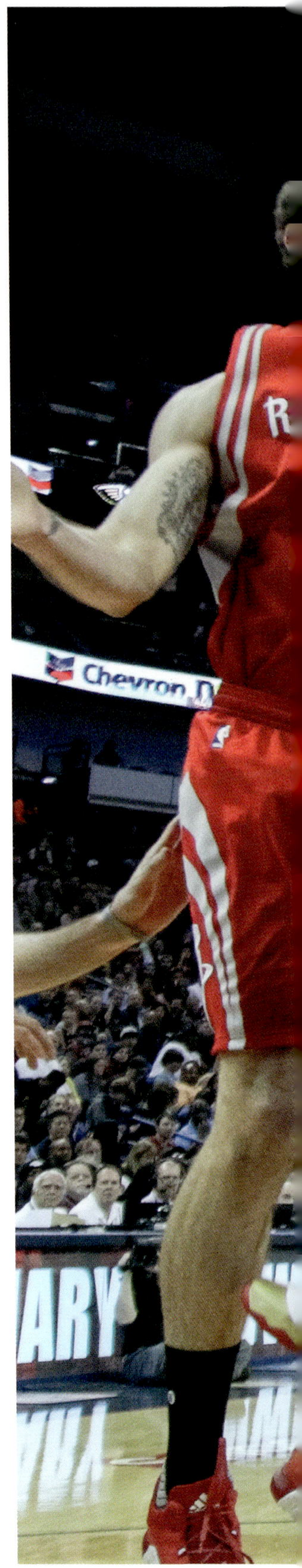

Swingman **TYREKE EVANS** helped the Pelicans cool down the Rockets in 2015.

LEGENDS OF THE HARDWOOD

AMERICA'S MUSIC

New Orleans is a port city. People from all over the world came there. Around 1900, the combination of European classical music, American blues, African rhythms, and South American song styles came together in a new musical form. It was called jazz. Some think *jazz* came from an African word for "energy, drive." Those words definitely describe jazz! Jazz musicians play music that's printed on a page. But they also make up tunes that go along with that music. This is called improvisation. During the Great Depression of the 1930s, many jazz musicians played swing music. It was lively and helped lift the spirits of Americans. New Orleans hoops have lived up to all those meanings.

easy points," said New Orleans power forward Ryan Anderson. "We just controlled the game for 48 minutes." He finished with 22 points. Evans added 21. The game was a big confidence builder for the Pelicans. It helped them earn a playoff berth later that year.

The history of pro basketball in New Orleans dates back about 50 years before that game. The New Orleans Buccaneers played in the American Basketball Association (ABA) from 1967 to 1970. The NBA granted the city an expansion franchise in 1974. Team officials named the new team the Jazz. "Jazz is one of those things for which New Orleans is nationally famous and locally proud," said co-owner Fred Rosenfeld. "It is a great art form which belongs to New Orleans and its rich history."

Unfortunately, the Jazz didn't make sweet music on the court. They won just 23 games in their first season. They had losing records the

"PISTOL" PETE MARAVICH thrilled fans with his dribbling, passing, and shooting.

next four seasons as well. The worst was 1978–79. The Jazz won only 26 games. One problem was New Orleans's Mardi Gras celebration. It took over the Louisiana Superdome for a month. The Superdome was the team's home court. So the Jazz couldn't play any home games in February. "A month on the road would put a crimp into anybody's win-loss record," said co-owner Sam Battistone.

One of the team's first big moves was trading for guard Pete Maravich. He set college records that no one has ever broken. In the 1976–77 season, Maravich led the NBA in scoring. He averaged more than 31 points a game. Unfortunately, Maravich suffered knee injuries the following season. By that time, fans were losing interest. The Jazz were having financial issues, too. In 1979, the team moved to Salt Lake City, Utah.

BUZZING INTO NEW ORLEANS

New Orleans wanted to replace the Jazz with another NBA team. In 1994, a local group tried to purchase the Minnesota Timberwolves. The deal almost went through. But it fell apart at the

Tiny guard **MUGGSY BOGUES** once blocked a shot by 7-foot center Patrick Ewing.

last minute. The Timberwolves stayed in Minnesota. In 2001, the Vancouver Grizzlies wanted to move. New Orleans made a bid for that team. So did the cities of Anaheim, California; Louisville, Kentucky; and Memphis, Tennessee. The Grizzlies chose Memphis.

A year later, the Charlotte Hornets also wanted a new home. Their name dated back to the Revolutionary War. But the Hornets didn't sting many opponents in their first season in 1988. The team lost its first game by 40 points. It won just 20 games that first season. Fans didn't seem to care. The Hornets led the league in attendance. One of the biggest attractions was the littlest player in NBA history: point guard Tyrone "Muggsy" Bogues. He stood just 5-foot-3! The Hornets did even worse in 1989–90. They only won 19 games. Charlotte improved to 26 wins the following season and 31 in 1991–92. Burly forward Larry Johnson was named Rookie of the Year.

LEGENDS OF THE HARDWOOD

HONORING A LOCAL HERO

UTAH JAZZ VS. NEW ORLEANS HORNETS, OCTOBER 30, 2002

Team officials wanted to show the connection between the present-day Hornets and the long-departed Jazz. A ceremony at halftime retired Pete Maravich's jersey number 7. The Utah Jazz had already done that, in 1985. "It's a wonderful honor," said Jackie Maravich, his widow. "I'm really happy to see his number in New Orleans." Maravich was named to the All-NBA First Team twice. One time he scored 68 points. "I'll never forget one particular play," said Hornets coach Paul Silas. "With one or two seconds to go, he let loose with this long hook shot. Then he just ran off toward the locker room and didn't even look to see if it went in. It hit bottom."

Quick shooting guard **DELL CURRY** sparked the team's offense off the bench.

Despite the losses, fans continued to flock to the Charlotte Coliseum. The Hornets rewarded that loyalty the following season. They won 44 games. They also defeated the Boston Celtics in the first round of the playoffs. But the Hornets lost to the New York Knicks in the next round. By then, another fan favorite had emerged. That was shooting guard Dell Curry. He was named Sixth Man of the Year in 1994. Curry still holds the Hornets' scoring record with 9,839 points.

Charlotte became a consistent winner. But the Hornets could never get past the second round of the playoffs. The team also had trouble holding on to its stars. Owner George Shinn demanded that the city build a new arena at no cost to him. The city refused. Attendance declined. The Hornets had the league's worst attendance in 2001–02. Even Shinn stopped going to games. He said he

Forward **JAMAL MASHBURN** led the Hornets in points per game for three years.

couldn't afford to keep the team in Charlotte. He wanted to move. New Orleans still wanted an NBA team. This time, the city didn't have any real competition. "I wanted the Hornets to stay in Charlotte," said Charlotte mayor Pat McCrory. "But the fact of the matter is we had an ownership team that made fans not want to come to ball games." As soon as the season ended, the team headed to New Orleans.

LEGENDS OF THE HARDWOOD

POINTING THE WAY TO STARDOM

CHRIS PAUL, POINT GUARD, 6 FEET, 2005–11

In high school, Chris Paul played junior varsity his first two seasons. As a junior, he led his team to the state semifinals. His grandfather was murdered during Paul's senior year. He was 61. To honor his memory, Paul scored 61 points in a game. He continued to shine at Wake Forest University. He helped the team achieve the nation's top ranking for two weeks during his sophomore year. It was the first time Wake Forest had ever been ranked so high. Paul was named a first-team All-American that season. He was also a first-team Academic All-American. He left Wake Forest when the season was over and made himself eligible for the NBA Draft.

STORMY TIMES

The Hornets' first game in their New Orleans home was a combination of past and present. They faced the Utah Jazz. That team had left New Orleans nearly 25 years earlier. The Hornets swarmed

Floor general **BARON DAVIS** scored plenty of points himself but was no ball hog.

Superstar **CHRIS PAUL** topped the NBA in assists and steals while with the Hornets.

"[CHRIS PAUL] HAS GREAT LEADERSHIP SKILLS," SAID GENERAL MANAGER ALLAN BRISTOW. "WE FEEL HE CAN BE A PART OF AN EXPLOSIVE YOUNG BACKCOURT FOR US."

the Jazz, winning 100–75. New Orleans continued to play well. Point guard Baron Davis and forward Jamal Mashburn become fan favorites. The Hornets finished the season 47–35. They lost to the Philadelphia 76ers in the first round of the playoffs.

The Hornets began the 2004–05 season by losing 29 of their first 31 games. They improved during the rest of the season but still finished with just 18 wins. It was the worst record in the team's history. There was a silver lining. The poor record meant the team had the fourth pick in the 2005 NBA Draft. With that pick, New Orleans took point guard Chris Paul. "He has great leadership skills," said general manager Allan Bristow. "We feel he can be a part of an explosive young backcourt for us." Unfortunately, it would be three years before fans got to see him play in New Orleans. Mother Nature was about to let loose her fury on the city.

On August 29, 2005, Hurricane Katrina pummeled New Orleans and the surrounding area. More than 2,000 people died in the storm and its aftermath. Massive floods put nearly 80 percent of the city under several feet of water. The Hornets couldn't play their home games in New Orleans. They had to relocate to Oklahoma City. That city wanted an NBA team. It had built the Ford Center in 2002 to be ready if the NBA expanded. Paul was certainly ready to play. He averaged 16 points and 8 assists a game. He led all rookies in scoring, assists, steals, total minutes played, double-doubles, and triple-doubles. He was the runaway winner of Rookie of the

Year honors. Third-year forward David West was an ideal addition to Paul's achievements. He averaged 17 points and more than 7 rebounds a game. The Hornets improved to 38 wins but didn't make the playoffs.

New Orleans still hadn't recovered from the storm in time for the 2006–07 season. So the Hornets stayed in Oklahoma City. They missed the playoffs again, winning 39 games. That didn't matter to fans. They kept filling up the Ford Center. Many people, including coach Byron Scott, wanted the Hornets to stay there permanently. "I would love to stay here and play in Oklahoma City next year," he said during the team's first season in Oklahoma. "I think our guys are at home here." The Oklahoma City fans were enthusiastic about "their" team. They treated players to free meals at restaurants. But the NBA didn't think it was a good idea. If the Hornets stayed in Oklahoma City, people might think the NBA was deserting the hard-hit city of New Orleans. It would create a lot of bad publicity for the league.

LEGENDS OF THE HARDWOOD

THE STARS SHINE ON NEW ORLEANS

NBA ALL-STAR GAME, NEW ORLEANS, FEBRUARY 27, 2008

The NBA wanted to help New Orleans recover from Hurricane Katrina. So the league scheduled the 2008 All-Star Game in the city. "I think the game helped New Orleans," said Sacramento Kings coach George Karl. Hornets fans were thrilled that point guard Chris Paul and forward David West both played in the game. Paul scored 16 points, dished out 14 assists, and had 4 steals. West netted six points. Both players also joined community service projects during the All-Star weekend. "It was something that really put basketball in prospective," said West. "It made us realize how real life can be."

Towering center **TYSON CHANDLER** used his size to grab rebounds and make soaring dunks.

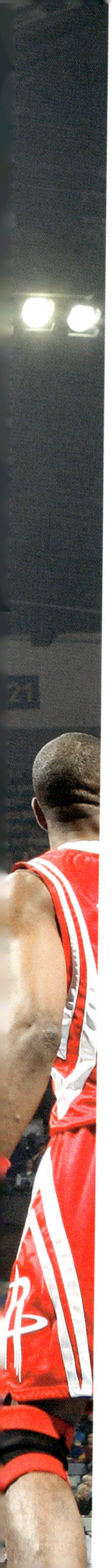

BACK TO THE BIG EASY

The Hornets returned to New Orleans, often called "The Big Easy," for the 2007–08 season. Players such as forward Peja Stojakovic and center Tyson Chandler provided scoring and defense. Paul was

The Pelicans' nest, New Orleans Arena, was renamed **SMOOTHIE KING CENTER** in 2014.

playing even better. The Hornets buzzed to a 56–26 mark for a franchise record. It was also the second-best record in the Western Conference. Only the Los Angeles Lakers did better. Scott was named Coach of the Year. New Orleans easily defeated the Dallas Mavericks in the first round of the playoffs, four games to one. The Hornets took a 3–2 lead in the second round over the defending NBA champion San Antonio Spurs. But they couldn't hold it. The Spurs won the two final games to take the series. New Orleans had another winning season the following year. The Hornets had 49 victories. The Denver Nuggets beat them in the first round of the playoffs, 4–1. After that, Chandler left the team. Paul was injured for half the 2009–10 season. The Hornets faltered without Chandler and Paul. They finished with a disappointing 37–45 mark.

They rebounded to win 46 games the following season. Once again, they lost in the first round of the playoffs. The biggest news happened off the court, though. For the second time in less than a decade, owner George Shinn was having financial problems. This time, he wanted to sell the team. One man wanted to buy the team and move it to California. The NBA didn't approve the sale. The league wanted to keep the Hornets in New Orleans. A local man made an offer, but it fell through. With time running out, the league decided to buy the team itself.

COMING CLOSE

NBA PLAYOFFS, GAME 7 OF THE SECOND ROUND, SAN ANTONIO SPURS AT NEW ORLEANS HORNETS, MAY 19, 2008

With a win, the Hornets would advance to the Western Conference finals. They fell behind by 15 points at the end of the third quarter. But fans didn't give up. They stood for the entire fourth quarter. The team didn't quit, either. Point guard Jannero Pargo drained a three-pointer to narrow the score to 83–80 with 90 seconds left. But the Spurs pulled away for a 91–82 victory. "One thing I want them to remember when they start working out next season is how they feel right now," said coach Byron Scott. "You have to go through some things before you can really understand how good it's going to feel when you get to that next level."

The 2011–12 season started late because of labor issues between owners and players. While that was going on, Paul was traded to the Los Angeles Clippers. Leaving the team was hard. "I was really a part of that city," Paul said. "I honestly can't say one negative thing about the city. If it were not for the city of New Orleans, I'm not who I am now. They just embrace you as family.... The trade happened at night, so it wasn't like you got to tell people bye. It happened, and we were gone." Without their best player, the Hornets struggled to a 21–45 mark. No one knew it at the time, but another superstar would soon be on his way to New Orleans.

FROM HORNETS TO PELICANS

In 2012, businessman Tom Benson bought the team. He also owned the New Orleans Saints. "There was concern by Mr. Benson that someone outside would buy this franchise [the Hornets] and try to move

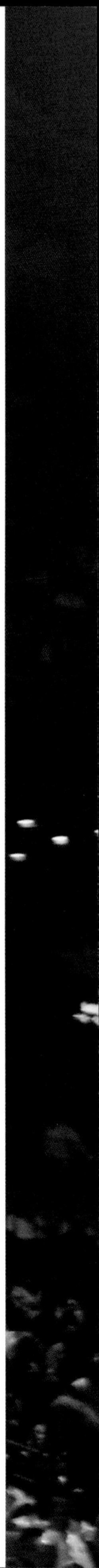

Guard **MARCUS THORNTON** provided solid offense in his short time in New Orleans.

LEGENDS OF THE HARDWOOD

UNDER THE RADAR

ANTHONY DAVIS, CENTER/POWER FORWARD, 6-FOOT-10, 2012–PRESENT

In high school, Anthony Davis played for Perspectives Charter School in Chicago. The academic-driven school didn't even have a gym. Most people dismissed him as "the little guy who would shoot threes from the corner." That was fine with him. "I wasn't going there because of basketball," Davis said. "My dream was always to go to college." Then he started growing. By his senior year, he stood 6-foot-10. He also starred on a traveling club team. Suddenly, people were interested in him. Davis realized his dream when he received a scholarship to the University of Kentucky. In his first year, he led the Wildcats to the national championship. He was named College Player of the Year.

it, and, to be quite honest, that was not what we wanted to do, because we had invested so much in this community," said team president Dennis Lauscha. Benson wanted to rename the team to showcase more local flavor. Jazz was his first choice. "Whether we can get that or let us use that, you've got to know we're working on it," he said. He offered to buy the name from Utah. Utah coach Ty Corbin said, "We can't give up our name." The team had too much history as the Jazz.

Benson decided on Pelicans. The brown pelican is the state bird of Louisiana. New Orleans sports historian S. Derby Gisclair said the name is "very emblematic because several years ago, brown pelicans were almost extinct. They made a comeback. New Orleans, after Hurricane Katrina, made *its* comeback."

Forward **AL-FAROUQ AMINU** had the strength and wingspan to pass tough opponents.

Shot-blocking big man **ANTHONY DAVIS** had great potential but struggled with injuries.

Charlotte had acquired a new team in 2004. It was called the Bobcats. Now the NBA made a deal with the two teams. New Orleans would become the Pelicans in 2013. Then Charlotte would take back the Hornets name in 2014. It would also reclaim the team's history from its 1988 founding to its departure for New Orleans. Accordingly, the Pelicans' official NBA history begins with the 2002–03 season.

About the same time Benson was finalizing the sale, the team's future arrived. That was burly power forward/center Anthony Davis. "AD"

Athletic guard **JRUE HOLIDAY** averaged 16.8 points and 6 assists per game in 2015–16.

had a sensational first year at the University of Kentucky. New Orleans took him as the top overall choice in the 2012 Draft. "New Orleans is a great city," Davis said. "When I came in, whatever I had to do to make everything go positively, I was more than willing and happy to do." In his first season, Davis scored 13.5 points and snagged 8 rebounds a game. He was named to the All-Rookie First Team. New Orleans wasn't as successful. It won only 27 games that season and 34 the next.

TYREKE EVANS averaged 15 points a game in 2015–16 but missed much of the season.

At 7-foot-2, French center **ALEXIS AJINCA** was a force around the rim.

"NEW ORLEANS IS A GREAT CITY," DAVIS SAID. "WHEN I CAME IN, WHATEVER I HAD TO DO TO MAKE EVERYTHING GO POSITIVELY, I WAS MORE THAN WILLING AND HAPPY TO DO."

The Pelicans returned to the winning column in 2014–15 with 45 wins. By then, it was obvious that AD would be one of the league's biggest stars. He was scoring well over 20 points and hauling in 10 rebounds a game. The Pelicans had the misfortune of playing the Golden State Warriors in the first round of the playoffs. The eventual NBA champions swept the series. New Orleans couldn't build on that success. The team won just 1 of its first 12 games in 2015–16 and finished 30–52. Another slow start and a season-long slew of injuries were too much for New Orleans in 2016–17. Despite adding two-time international gold medalist and NBA All-Star center DeMarcus Cousins in a late-season trade, the Pelicans could manage only a 34–48 mark.

The Pelicans have survived shaky ownership and weathered one of the worst natural disasters in American history. Now they have put down solid roots under equally solid ownership. Fans hope that the team will soon do what the Saints already have: bring a championship trophy home to the Big Easy.

SELECTED BIBLIOGRAPHY

Ballard, Chris. *The Art of a Beautiful Game: The Thinking Fan's Tour of the NBA*. New York: Simon & Schuster, 2010.

Hareas, John. *Ultimate Basketball: More Than 100 Years of the Sport's Evolution*. New York: DK, 2004.

Hubbard, Jan, ed. *The Official NBA Basketball Encyclopedia*. 3rd edition. New York: Doubleday, 2000.

NBA.com. "New Orleans Pelicans." http://www.nba.com/pelicans.

Simmons, Bill. *The Book of Basketball: The NBA According to the Sports Guy*. New York: Ballantine, 2009.

Sports Illustrated. *Sports Illustrated Basketball's Greatest*. New York: Sports Illustrated, 2014.

WEBSITES

JR. NBA
http://jr.nba.com/

This kids site has games, videos, game results, team and player information, statistics, and more.

JR. PELICANS KIDS CLUB
http://www.nba.com/pelicans/jrpelicans

Check out the official Pelicans Kids Club website for fan gear and more for ages 13 and under.

Note: Every effort has been made to ensure that any websites listed above were active at the time of publication. However, because of the nature of the Internet, it is impossible to guarantee that these sites will remain active indefinitely or that their contents will not be altered.

INDEX